Little Wolf,
Pack Leader

Also by Ian Whybrow
and illustrated by Tony Ross

Little Wolf's Book of Badness
Little Wolf's Diary of Daring Deeds
Little Wolf's Haunted Hall for Small Horrors
Little Wolf, Forest Detective
Dear Little Wolf
Little Wolf's Handy Book of Poems

First American edition published in 2003 by Carolrhoda Books, Inc.

Text copyright © 2002 by Ian Whybrow
Illustrations copyright © 2002 by Tony Ross

Published by arrangement with HarperCollins Publishers Ltd, London, England.
Originally published in English by HarperCollins Publishers Ltd under the title
LITTLE WOLF, PACK LEADER

The author and illustrator assert the moral right to be identified as the author
and illustrator of the work.

Carolrhoda Books, Inc.
A division of Lerner Publishing Group
241 First Avenue North
Minneapolis, MN 55401 U.S.A.

Website address: www.lernerbooks.com

Library of Congress Cataloging-in-Publication Data

Whybrow, Ian.
Little Wolf, pack leader / by Ian Whybrow ; illustrated by Tony Ross.— 1st American ed.
        p.   cm.
Summary: In letters home to Mom and Dad, Little Wolf describes his new pack, the
Beastshire SPOBBTHALOF (Small Pack of Brute Beasts That Have a Load of Fun.)
ISBN: 1–57505–400–0 (lib. bdg. : alk. paper)
[1. Wolves—Fiction. 2. Brothers—Fiction. 3. Mystery and detective stories.]
I. Ross, Tony, ill. II. Title.
PZ7.W6225 Lh 2003
[Fic]—dc21   2002008774

Manufactured in the United States of America
1 2 3 4 5 6 – SB – 08 07 06 05 04 03

Little Wolf,
Pack Leader

Ian Whybrow

Illustrated by Tony Ross

Carolrhoda Books, Inc., Minneapolis

For Oisín Twomey Brenner,
who sometimes reads books for his dad

Dear Mom and Dad,

You say in your letter how is our darling baby pet, hmmm? I am kwite well thank you for not asking, hem hem, I know you mean Smellybreff really.

Answer: Smells is his usual small painy self. He has got a new craze. It is being a rock star on the drums. Today he is all whiny just because I took my saucepans from him for going *dink donk* on them with his hammer and lectric drill.

Smells said I must give him loads of gold for buying him a rock star suit plus real drums. But I said, "Gold, what gold? Who was the 1 who blew up my safe with gunpowder so my gold went *chinkle plonk* all over Frettnin Forest? It was YOU!"

Now he is out in the Forest having a look with his metal detector, saying he will be rich soonly, so nah nah.

Can you take him back to the Lair with you, please pleeeeze PLEEEEEEEEZ? You know you miss him, yesss?

Yours hopingly,

Little Wolf (son)

Dear Mom and Dad,

Your note sounds a small bit grrrrrish about me letting Smells go out by himself. I do not know Y, he comes indoors when he is starving (e.g., a lot). Beeeeesides, you always say to give in to him, it is the only way.

Also you say you will not be taking him back just now, but let you know if he has any luck with his metal detector, then you might just change your mind.

Now I will say my
news. We are a bit short
of snacks here (not
many rabbits in
Frettnin Forest any
more, boo shame).
Yeller (best friend and
cuz) is not staying with
me in my house. He
has gone off southly for
a rabbit hunt and
private Lone Wolf

practiss. I miss his cheery shouting. It is very
quiet, except for Smells whining.

Normus Bear has gone away huntingly 2, only
not southly. He is more westly so he can tickle
trouts (not rabbits) out of Spring River down the

valley by Lonesome Woods, Murkshire. Plus looking privately for a nice hibernaty cave for snoozing in when the snow comes. I miss his rufftuff ways.

Stubbs has knitted himself a nice twiggy nest on the roof. He thinks he can fly better if he starts from high up.

I can hear him going "Ark" to the big crows sometimes, but I do not see him a lot like I used to, only when he has a small *ark*sident and falls down the chimney hole.

Mom, any rabbit rolls you can spare?

Yours hintingly,

Petit Starver (French)

The Big Old Place that Used to Belong to Uncle Bigbad, FRETTNIN FOREST, BEASTSHIRE!

Down in the garden

Dear Mom and Dad,

I got a postcard from Normus today saying wish you were hairy (joke). He says he is having a nice time, only a bit 2 much trout maybe. Also no luck with caves.

You say you have got new ~~naybores~~, ~~nayboors~~, people next door called Fang and Mauler Snarl-Wolfington—they sound cool, but are they nice noisy wuns?

Yours interestedly,

L. Wolf

The Bathroom

Dear Mom and Dad,

Yeller says Arrrrrroooo in a short note to let me know he has made himself cozy in a nice smelly hole, not 2 sunny in the morningtime. It is a good place for having new ideas about funny tricks, ect.

Here is a good 1 he sent me for tricking your mom. Go into the bathroom, get some toilet paper, go around and around with it till you are covered up, then shout, "Mummy! Mummy!"

If your mommy comes along wurrid, saying, "Yes?" then you say (hollow voice) "So am I, har har!"

13

Here is my Cheesy Toothpaste trick I sent him back. Get sum Skweezy Cheesy in a tube, cross out the words on it saying "Skweezy Cheesy" and put "Toothpaste." Then if your dad says, "Hey, stop brushing your teeth all the time!" you say, "Har Har, I am eating cheese really."

Yours chucklingly,

Little

P.S. For this toothpaste trick you can use any old tube of food like condensed milk, but not glue, Ok? (Bit harsh.)

Dear Mom and Dad,

Thank you for your gruff letter saying stop tricking and start hunting for a ~~nowrushing~~ ~~newrishing~~ murishing joosy snack for your poor little sweetypaws, Smells. You do not menshun my tummy, which has gone small as a small ant. Never mind, off I go suddenly to fetch Smells a nice fat moosy or a buffalo, maybe. So do not blame me if he gets gassy like normal for not chewing proply.

Yours,

A. Noid

Dear Mom and Dad,

Thank you for the nice pic of the cool new people next door that Dad took with his new spy camera strapped to his knee.

Shame he did not tuck the camera up higher. I like pics with faces on them. Never mind.

You say their lair has 5 sleepholes and 2 lickrooms, plus they have a really really really clever cub called Spoiler who knows EVERYTHING.

Plus, you say he is a real brute beast, not a small weaky like me who only likes reading and writing.

Now I am all upset.

Yours jealously,

Littly

P.S. Do not tell Spoiler any of our tricks, case he steals them, Ok?

P.P.S. Smells has just come in all wet but still no gold.

P.P.P.S. Yes, I am going to give him some grub NOW. It is my hedgehog. I was saving it as a treat 4 me, but never mind.

Dear Mom and Dad,

Not fair you sending Smellybreff that package
with the spanking machine in it, just because you
say I am not a real brute beast. Also, the machine
was batteries not included. So Smells has stolen
all of mine out of my flashlight, my Walkwolf,
and my swimmy bathfrog, ect. Just so the
machine would chase me around going
Swish bonk ow.

Also, thanks for your crool postcard that you
sent saying serve you right plus instruckshuns.
All right, I will look after Smells for ages more,
but tell him to stop being a fusspot, saying
he only likes eating Krispy Ducklets with
Moosepops, also skweezing gravy in the
keyholes, not funny.

Yours warmbottomly,

L. Wolf

P.S. I hope those batteries wear out soon, Ow.

Dear Mom and Dad,

Thank you for your moany reply, very newsy but damp. (Smells dropped it down the toilet, so cubbish.) It was kwite hard reading it with lots of the ink gone spready.

You say you are absolutely dis-something (is it custard?) because of the Snarl-Wolfingtons being so fancy and rich and us only poorish now.

Also, you say you are fed up about them always boasting about their son Spoiler. He is getting faymuss by being Pack Leader of his own fearsum wolfpack and him only 3 times my age and bigness.

Y is he always getting his pic in *Wolf Weekly* for facing something I cannot read? Is it clanger or dancer? No wait, it might be DANGER he keeps facing. Oh, I get it.

You say what about me? "Have you done anything for us to have a good boast about?" Answer: YES, I am giving Uncle Bigbad's big old house a fine straightening! Plus I am being a good cubsitter for Smells and letting him eat all my snowy weather snacks.

More tomorrowly,

Busyboy

Dear Mom and Dad,

Before, I was feeling a little downinthedumper so I thought, hey, best thing if you are onyourownly is think of a new fun thing to do.

So phew, yesterday I got all Uncle Bigbad's bits and pieces together that he had in this big old ~~manshun~~ ~~mantyion~~ house before he died of the jumping beanbangs! (All the beds out of the bedroom, the desks, the blackboards, ect.) I put them all in a couple of rooms upstairs. Then I did a fancy sign on the door saying, L. Wolf's Interesting Museum

Today I am making a place for all the
adventure stuff that me and Yeller had when we
turned Cunning College into Adventure Academy.
(I had 1 quick go on the zipwire, just 4 luck.)

W H E E E -
BONK!

Next I will make a place in the cellar for all our Haunted Hall stuff we had when we were teaching small brutes haunty tricks, *wooooo*.

Then, after, I will make 1 more place for all our Forest Detective Agency fingerprint kits, magnifying glasses, ect.

Guess what I will be then? A museum keeper! Loads of brute beasts will love to have a rummage in Uncle Bigbad's old house, plus have a laugh with his small naughty nephew, I bet!

Yours rushaboutly,

Little

L. Wolf's Interesting Museum
The Big Old Place that Used to
Belong to Uncle Bigbad,
FRETTNIN FOREST, BEASTSHIRE

Dear Mom and Dad,

You say museums are stupid, also stop that sissy
tidying, it is no good for boasting about. But I am
not tidying, I told you, I am straightening.

You say it is still all my fault
that Mr. and Mrs. Snarl-
Wolfington keep blabbing
about their son, Spoiler. And
now he has an RV all of his
ownly. You say Y cannot I be
all mature like him? I 'spect
you are jealous, just because
of him buying it out of his
own pocket money that his Gran
gave him for being "a credit to his long family
name." Not fair, blaming me if he keeps driving
splashingly through puddles near you saying,
"Good wun, yah?"

Anyhow, I do not have a pocket to put Granny money in. Plus, you know I do not even have a Granny, not since she got her temper up and ate herself.

Yours chindownly,

Little

P.S. What is RHYWP?

Dear Mom and Dad,

Thank you for your crool news about some lucky wolves having oldest cubs to be proud of. True I have not got an RV or a pack of my own. BUT (big but) I am giving in to Smells, plus I am better at reading and joined-up writing than their oldest cub, I bet.

Also, you say that RHYWP stands for **R**eally **H**arsh **Y**oung **W**olf **P**ack and that Spoiler is getting ready to drive his RV to Frettnin Forest and camp!

What a big head he has! Frettnin Forest has got enuff proud wolves, called me and Smells. So if he comes parking himself, I will have a good spy of his harsh habits, then I will see him off, no messing. I will say (rumbly voice), "Hey, you, buzz off out of our forest, OK yah?" Then he will think, "Oh no, sorry, we are trespassing on Little Wolf's land, he sounds strong and tuff. Adios."

Yours shockingly,

L. Wolf (Gold Badness Badge)

Dear Mom and Dad,

You know I put up that sign on my front door
saying Interesting Museum, ect., the other day?
Well, guess what? *Today* I had a visitor. She was a
little old lady in a bonnet and she had gingery
whiskers plus a peppery smell. Also she was
interested in seeing if there was a big safe with
gold in it from the days when Uncle Bigbad had
Cunning College. Then she
looked into my eyes
and I felt a little
swimmy in the
head, then off
she went swiftly
so I did not see
her any more,
boo shame.

Plus, remember what I said about not many rabbits? Now I have found out Y. It is Mister Twister the Fox and Master of Dizgizzes (still cannot spell it). He has been capturing loads of them with a crafty poster stuck by nail to many a tree in Frettnin Forest. I am sending you 1.

Yours, ly,

Little Wolf

P.S. Clever trick, huh? But whyo Y does he want to steal them all? There are way 2 many for 1 crafty fox to eat!

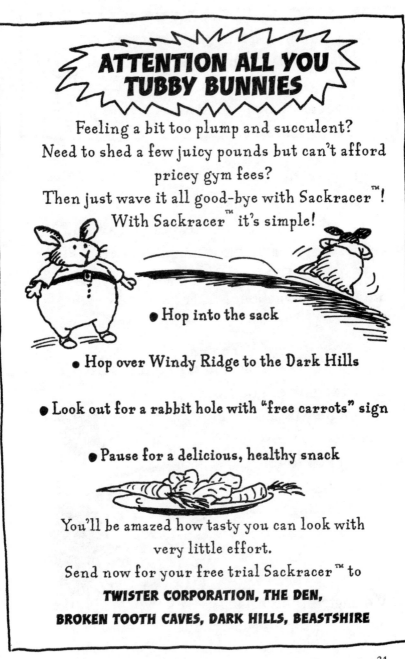

ATTENTION ALL YOU TUBBY BUNNIES

Feeling a bit too plump and succulent?
Need to shed a few juicy pounds but can't afford pricey gym fees?
Then just wave it all good-bye with Sackracer™!
With Sackracer™ it's simple!

- Hop into the sack

- Hop over Windy Ridge to the Dark Hills

- Look out for a rabbit hole with "free carrots" sign

- Pause for a delicious, healthy snack

You'll be amazed how tasty you can look with very little effort.
Send now for your free trial Sackracer™ to
**TWISTER CORPORATION, THE DEN,
BROKEN TOOTH CAVES, DARK HILLS, BEASTSHIRE**

31

Dear Mom and Dad,

Thank you for the nice fearsum pic of Dad
saying, "Forget about that museum or else." Plus,
the extra GRRRRS you sent for me saying
Yours ✍ ly about Mister Twister. Now I
am all out of breath by repeating, "I must not be
impressed by foxy tricks, they are dumb,"
1 millium times. Plus, you say I must HURRY
UP and think of good ways
to capture Mister Twister
quick, just because he
is a big Foe to us
wolves. Also, so I can
claim the huge reward
and send it to you,
yes? Then you can be
rich like the Snarl-
Wolfingtons, plus having a
Number 1 son to boast about.

I have had a good study of that reward poster you sent of Mister Twister ~~in his latest dis-skies dussgize~~ dressed up. I will try my tuffest to capture him, but it will be a hard job I bet because of so many trees around here just like him.

Yours keenly,

L. B. Wolf

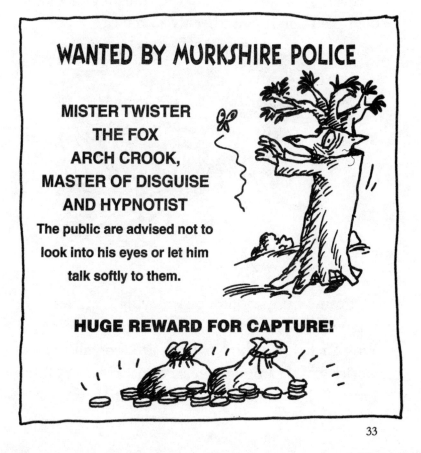

WANTED BY MURKSHIRE POLICE

**MISTER TWISTER
THE FOX
ARCH CROOK,
MASTER OF DISGUISE
AND HYPNOTIST**
The public are advised not to
look into his eyes or let him
talk softly to them.

HUGE REWARD FOR CAPTURE!

The Bedroom

Dear Mom and Dad,

Guess what woke me up this morning? A loud Blah Blah coming southeastly to my ears.

It came from a loudshouter saying, "Spoiler calling, Pack Leader of The Really Harsh Young Wolf Pack, OK yah? Now pay attention all you weaky wolves around here, and that means YOU, Little Wolf. You have been far too soft, letting

Mr. Twister get away with his criminal behavior for so long, yah? All right, listen up! I and my RHYWP intend to put that fox in a box pretty darn quick, understand?

"So if you want to be part of the action, trot yourselves over to my RV on the north shore of Lake Lemming and get some real training. I am prepared to train you in Harshness, Tracking, Being More Crafty than Foxes, and Capturing. If you obey orders and accept me as your Pack Leader, I might even let you have a little tiddly bit of the HUGE REWARD I intend to earn from turning Mr. Twister over to the police. Now get a move on! Because if you don't come to us on the double, we will come and fetch you!

No matter how deep you dig, we'll come and pull you out of your hidy-hole by your teeny, tiny tail, I kid you not, yah? Roger and Out."

You know Uncle Bigbad used to say, "Blinking Blunker?" Well I think Spoiler is 1. He made all my neckhairs get stiffed up. Out of bed I jumped rushingly to give him a sharp seeing off! Only I could not go straight over because I had to wait for Smells to put on his engine driver outfit plus oily rag. Not fair, just because his small brane thinks training goes *woo woo chuff chuff*.

Never mind, ready now, off we go!

Yours sternly,

L. Bad Wolf,
Son of Gripper

Dear Mom and Dad,

Now I will say my news about Smells and me
arriving at Lake Lemming shore. He was sad
because of no trains but he got more cheery
because I let him put a rubber duck on his head
and go in the reeds to do spying with me
crawlingly.

1st we met some birds (they were
kwite tasty). Then on the shore we
spied Spoiler doing camping with his Really
Harsh Young Wolf Pack. Spoiler has got many a
big snarler in his pack. They are big huge cubs,
more like dad-size, really. I like the uniform they
wear, it is tracksuity (shadow color), plus big
writing on the back saying RHYWP.

You can tell which one is Spoiler. He is the biggest 1 with the dark glasses on plus a SPOILER, PACK LEADER T-shirt.

His best saying is, "Listen up, guys!" in a hot-shot way of bossing around. He makes his pack call him PL. Like, if they hear him say an order, they have to say back, "OK yah, PL, great idea!" They all like jogging bunchedupply along by the shore, singing ambush songs.

Yours spyingly,

Quack (code name)

P.S. We are going to mail this and then have another spy after.

Dear Mom and Dad,

Today we got ambushed, all because of Smells being a hopeless spy.

Spoiler's pack came over to the lake for a poke around in the reeds. I said whisperingly, "Quick, Smells, make some duck noises," and he went "woof woof **moo moo**." So selfish.

Did I say about the lectric fence? Well I am inside it. Also I am in a small secret cell, but not sure what happened to Smells except I can hear him saying, "yah yah yah" all the time.

Yours lockedinly,

L.W.

Dear Mom and Dad,

Now I will say about the inside of the RV. It has a driving part in the front plus all cozy in the back, a bit like normal lairs but more modern with loads of lectric things going *hmmm*. For example, a fridge full of Moosejoose in the kitchen (yum, yes please). There is a bathroom and lickroom, plus nice dark smelly corners for curlups. Plus, it has this cell I am kept in behind a secret panel and only Spoiler knows the combination to open it. The outside of the RV is all armor-plated with a

lectric fence going around outside, so hard to
have a sneaky peep in.

Spoiler gave me a hard arm burn saying,
"Come on, give in, say 'You are my Pack Leader
and I want to join the RHYWP and be trained
by you!'" But I said, "No way, never never, ect."
Plus I was not trembly at all, hardly.

Yours stubbornly,

L. Wolf

P.S. Ooo-ow my arm.

Dear Mom and Dad,

Today, Spoiler did "Get Your Mussels Up" with his pack by chewing rocks, push-ups, running, ect.

Also, he made the RHYWP do Harshness tests like Jump in the Lake till you turn Blue, plus Backbiting, Ripping, Insulting, ect.

Not fair. Grinder, Biff, Gray, and Sleek keep saying I am a small sissy, plus I am 2 humble to be in their pack anyway. Also, I heard Grabber tell Smoke that I did not come out of the Top Drawer or go to a Top School so poo-poo to me.

So I said, "Maybe not, but here is a Top Insult. You come out of my Top Drawer, you are underwear har har!" But they did not laugh—so moody.

They keep making a big fuss of Smells, going *pat pat tickle tickle,* but not right now with the sun falling in the water. Right now they are all looking at a big map momblingly, saying, "Mister Twister, Mister Twister, abslootly, deffnly, we'll get the booger, BIG money reward, OK no sweat, yah?"

Yours listeningly,

A. Left (new code name)

Dear Mom and Dad,

   Guess what? I am freeeeeeeee, Spoiler uncaptured me! First he made me listen to his pack howling Ambush Songs till after the gong of midnight. The words are dumb but I will put 1 down for you in fancy writing anyhow.

Spoiler is our Leader, hey!
We are harsh and we don't care!
Our Wolf Pack is Number 1!
We know how to spoil your fun!

We like taking it in turns,
To give weakies bad arm burns.
Listen up and listen good!
We can bite through lumps of wood.

Really Harsh Young Wolves are we,
The Hairy Scary WP!
This is tuff but this is true
We have ways to capture you!

Mister Twister, you're no good,
You are just a spindly dude!
Mister Twister can't you see,
You can't hide from the WP!

PUSH! PUSH! AMBUSH!

But all I kept saying bravely was, "You cannot scare me in my own forest. You are just big snobs and bullies! I am L. Wolf, Son of Gripper, Nephew of Bigbad, grrrr, ect."

So in the end Spoiler came tapping in the combination that undid the lock of my secret cell. He let me out, saying, "Oh, go away, you teeny fluffball, we are not wasting our time training you. Trot along and don't come back till you've grown some fur on your chest, you hear? I've got *important* brute beasts to capture, like Mister Twister for a start, so it's time for me to take a little looksee.

"Hey, and remember, your baby brother is with me now. So don't try any of your tricks to stop me earning my huge reward, OK yah? Or Smellybreff might get upset in a BIG way, you follow?"

Grinder, Biff, Gray, and Sleek gave me an arm burn each for luck. Then the RHYWP packed up the lectric fence, jumped in the RV, and off they drove quick with headlights on.

Yours sorewristly,

L. Wolf

P.S. I forgot to say about Smells. Spoiler has let him tie himself to the radiator of his RV, so he can be a mascot. Now he will have a thrill and let Spoiler be his Pack Leader—so shaming for his big brother.

Dear Mom and Dad,

2 much awakeness last night, now I am soooo tired and upset.

It is not because of so many arm burns, but I did not like them laughing plus calling me small fluffball. I chased after the RV but my legs do not go around as fast as wheels, so no good. Then I sat pantingly in the blackness saying to me (big breff), "Listen, you are all on your ownly, your friends are faraway, your baby bro has gone off with harsh strangers. Plus you are in the middle of a dark damp forest, nothing 2 eat, no flashlight. Now have a think. What would Mom and Dad do now?"

Answer: # HOWL!

So I did. Quick as a chick I ran and ran through Frettnin Forest, in and out of the deep shadows howling, "HELP! HELP!" and "WHERE ARE YOU, SMELLS?" Sad to say I was just going around and around, banging into trees.

Also tripping over roots with my breff hot in my throat, seeing fat monsters and slimy spooks everywhere. Then I got dizzy, so I fell over and bonked my head.

Your sorry boy,

Littly

Dear Mom and Dad,

Guess who found me and stitched a nice quilt
of dry leaves with his clever beak for warmness?
Stubbs! All because of a small crowd of crows I
woke up in the nighttime with my howling.
They flew south past Stubby's nest on the roof of
my house the next day and said to him crowly
about me going Help *Bonk*.

So Stubbs said "Ark!" meaning *Ark*shun
Stations, and did his best flying looking 4 me.
But when he did not see fluff nor fur of me, back
he flew to Frettnin Forest. Good thing, because
he found me at the top edge of it, curled up dead
nearly.

I said, "I am so shamed, Stubbs, I have let down the name of Wolf by losing Smells to the RHYWP." But he said, "Ark!" meaning Open your be*ark*. Then he gave me a good snack of chewy wigglers he found eating a treestump. So now I am all strong again. I am going to sit him on my head most of the way home (saves wings) but he can flap up above the trees now and then for a look, in case of me going the wrong way.

Yours homewardly,

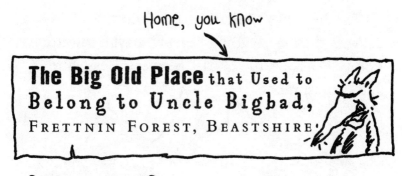

Home, you know

The Big Old Place that Used to **Belong to Uncle Bigbad,** FRETTNIN FOREST, BEASTSHIRE

Dear Mom and Dad,

Me and Stubbs had another chat today, me all cozy in bed, him on the windowsill. It was *ark*cellent. I told him all about Spoiler and his RV and how he has Smells as his mascot (so shaming for his big brother). Stubbs said, "Ark! Ark!" meaning *Ark*tually, he saw some wheely tr*ark*s when he was looking for me flying flappingly, 1st eastly over the River Riggly as far as Hazardous Canyon.

But the trarks were not going into the
canyon, they were going northly maybe toward
Pointy Peaks on the border between Beastshire
and Grimshire.

Maybe the RHYWP are going toward the
White Wildness and Yellowsmoke Swamplands or
to Vile Isle, but they are not going the short way
like crows fly!

Then I got all sadly because even though
Smells is a ~~noosance~~ ~~newsance~~ pest he is still my
baby bro. But he will never want to be with me
now, I bet, boo shame. I am 2 unthrilly with no
RV radiator to tie himself on to.

Stubbs said, "Ark!" meaning B*ark* yourself up!
That is enuff Sorry for Yourselfness!

I said, "Yes, but not
fair being just 1 small
wolf vs. Spoiler plus all
his harsh RHYWPs!"

Stubbs said back, "Ark" times
3! meaning I hope you are
being s*ark*astic, because what
about Stubby Crow,
*Ark*sqwire, plus your 2 other
rem*ark*able chums?"

I said, "Do you think Yeller and Normus
would give up their private time just to come
and help me?" Stubbs answered, "Ark!" meaning
Ark you kidding? Course they would!

Your hopeful boy,

Little

The Big Old Place that Used to **Belong to Uncle Bigbad,** FRETTNIN FOREST, BEASTSHIRE

Dear Mom and Dad,

Off went Stubbs today after double worms for his br*ark*fast. I gave him a good launch off the roof with our new Crowspeeder we made 'specially.

If his wings are good flappers, maybe he can deliver 2 arkmails in 1 single day, saying:

Emerjuncy shock. Come back to my house quick, I need your help! A strange pack of hot-shot wolves has turned Smells's head. I must go and get him back by hick or by trick. Sorry for ~~inconveen inconveinyunce~~ screwing up your vacation,
Your friendly,
L.B.W.

Then I got out my detective stuff from the museum. See, it was good having that straightening! Plus my backpack, maps, tent, ect. for a dustoff. Also Smells's teddy bear, in case he wants to be my baby bro again. I shall practiss my hicks and tricks and tracking, for I must be off soonly and find Spoiler. He needs showing who is Top Wolf of Beastshire, huff puff!

Yours Big Badly,

Little

55

The Big Old Place that Used to Belong to Uncle Bigbad,
FRETTNIN FOREST, BEASTSHIRE

Dear Mom and Dad,

Arrrooo!!! Normus has come already with loads of trouts for snacks. Nice, but they give you a coff from all the hairy bones. When I opened the door 4 him, he gave me a hard bearhug saying, "Good to see you, Littly. Trout tickling is fun but not good fun like bashing. Don't you get wurrid! Where is that hot-shot wolfpack of strangers? Let me go and give them a hard punching!"

I said I did not know xactly where they went but they were looking for Mister Twister out eastly. Normus said, "Imagine those Harshies turning Smells's head around! That is so crool! He is only a small teddycub!"

You know I said in my arkmails the RHYWP has turned Smells's head? Well Normus does not understand sayings. He thinks they really have turned Smells's head around the other way. Never mind, it is nice he wants to help so much, right? But where is Yeller and where is Stubbs? Uh-oh, I hope Spoiler has not caught them by trick or trap.

Yours ankshussly,

Little

Dear Mom and Dad,

My best news is about Yeller. He has come at last. Bit slow, but not his fault and no tricking or trapping by Spoiler, arrrooooo! Stubbs was so weak from his arkstra long fly, 1st westly then southly, Yeller had to do 1st aid on him by sticking him in his shirt for a warmup. Plus feed him mushy peabugs by eyedropper.

Yeller said, "HELLO LICKLE! HOW'S TRICKS?" Then he gave me a funny pawshake with his arm going, "Tootle-toot!" (Not really, it was a false skweezy 1, he had it on for a joke!) Then we had loads of rabbit rolls he brought from down south, yes please, yum yum. Plus saving all the chewy bits for Stubbs to get his strongness up. Yeller said loudly how he liked being private for short times, 'specially if there are rabbits handy. But more fun is helping your chums find the RHYWP and Mr. Twister. Plus thinking of Big Ideas and tricks for fixing problems together. We are all 2 tired out for talking now, but we will know what to do by tomorrow, I bet, by having a good powwow.

Yours feelingbetterly,

Little

Dear Mom and Dad,

Do not fret and frown, we will soon have Smells back. Probly.

I told the chums about Spoiler, how he thinks he is Top Wolf not just in Murkshire where my Mom and Dad live (that is you, just in case you are not sure, OK?) but even here in Beastshire. Also I xplained about the bigness of his harsh wolfpack, plus his RV going a lot quicker than wolf cubs. Then I told them about getting captured, plus Smells going away with the RHYWP to be their mascot.

Quick as a chick they all wanted to go and fight Spoiler. Yeller said loudly, "POOR OLD LICKLE, SO SHAMIN FOR YOUR PROUD NAME OF WOLF! LET ME HELP YOU. Y DON'T WE RUSH AFTER THEM AND DO A SHOCKIN TRICK ON SPOILER?"

I said, "Thank you, so kind. Plus, we must capture Mister Twister before Spoiler does, so we can get the huge reward."

Yeller said, "NO NEED TO GET WURRID ABOUT SPOILER GETTIN THERE FIRST, LICKLE! NOBODY KNOWS WHERE MISTER TWISTER LIVES. HEY! WAIT A SEC! I KNOW WHERE THERE MIGHT BE A GOOD CLUE! LET'S GO AND HAVE ANOTHER LOOK AT HIS TRICK POSTER FOR GETTIN RABBICKS TO JUMP INTO SACKS!"

So off we went pantingly to a tree with the bunny poster on it. And yes, it says on the poster about hop along to Windy Ridge! Also, it has an address in Broken Tooth Caves on the bottom! Arrrrrooo for Yeller!

Your cheery boy,

Little

Dear Mom and Dad,

You know I did that cheery arrrroooo in my last note? Sorry, that came out a bit 2 quick. Because Normus, Yeller, and Stubbs keep forgetting 1 thing. I said, "I know my name Wolf is just a short 1, not like Snarl-Wolfington, but I must not let Spoiler keep doing more daring deeds than me, or I will let that name right down. It is me must get Smells back, plus capture Mr. Twister, not you."

Then Normus said buttinly, "Oh, no, Little, this job is much too big for 1 small wolfcub. You say Spoiler and the RHYWP are gnashing for a bashing. They are big and harsh, so bashing them is the only way, with harder biting and arm burns. They have all got miles bigger mussels than you. I will go and do the bashing, you know I like it."

I said, "No, Normus. I have to be a lone wolf and do it all on my ownly, or Mom and Dad will say: Nar Nar bubbacub, You are just a blubbercub!"

Then Stubbs said, "Ark!" meaning, Stop *ark*uing. I will fly high up and drop crowstuff on Spoiler's head, plus his RHYWP. Yeller said, "WHAT SORT OF STUFF, STUBBY?" Stubbs said, "Ark!" meaning I'll whisp*ark*. Then Yeller said, "OH, I SEE, THAT SORT OF STUFF. YEAH, WELL, THAT WOULD BE GOOD, BUT BETTER IF YOU COULD TEACH A BIG HERD OF ELEPHANTS FLYIN, HAR HAR!"

It is nice to have a laugh, even if you are feeling more low than a worm's belly button.

Yours notsureyettly,

Little

Special thinky spot, under chair by my desk

Dear Mom and Dad,

Something proud happened to me today, here it is.

Our powwows have been loooooooooooong wuns with many a "Trouble is" in them.

I will say Yeller's latest loud "Trouble is" for you. He said, "TROUBLE IS, HAVIN THE RHYWP MEANS THAT SPOILER HAS GOT EYES AND EARS EVERYWHERE. HE HAS GOT MANY A WET NOSE TO SNIFF WITH, PLUS LOADS OF LEGS TO RUN WITH, PLUS HUNDREDS OF TEETH TO BITE WITH. NO LONE BRUTE CAN DEFEAT HIM, LICKLE. ONLY A WOPPIN BIG STRONG WOLFPACK WILL DO IT—AND WHERE WILL WE FIND WUN IN ALL THIS LAND?"

I was all upset, BUT (big but), just then, a fine thought jumped in my head. *Ding!* I said, "Maybe we cannot find a **wopping big strong** wolfpack! But I think I know where to find a **Special** sort of pack, with only a few brute beasts in it maybe, but brave and smart!"

All the chums jumped up saying, "Where, where, where?"

And I said answeringly, "Right here, because that Special pack is US!"

Your braney boy,

Me (Clue: not any of the others)

Dear Mom and Dad,

Here is my new news about that Special pack I said about. Normus was a bit wurrid saying, "But Little, what about bear cubs? Packs are only for wolves, aren't they?"

I said, "Not our Special pack, Normus, you can be in ours!" So he said OK, he wanted to join and do some dyb-dob-dybbing.

Still, Stubbs was not sure, saying, "Ark!" meaning *ark*scuse me, how can crowchicks be in packs?

I said, "Easy cheesy, you just say you want to be IN!" So he said, "Ark!" meaning *Ark*-kay, he wanted to.

Yeller shouted, "YOW, I LIKE THIS IDEA, I'M JOININ 2 AND I HAVE THOUGHT UP A GOOD NAME FOR OUR PACK. WE CAN BE CALLED SPOBB, SHORT FOR **S**MALL **P**ACK **O**F **B**RUTE **B**EASTS."

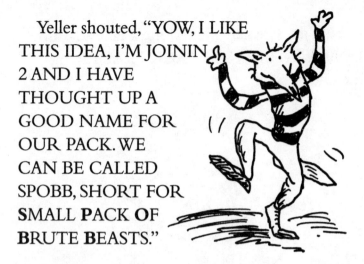

Then Normus said hopingly, "Are we going to be Harsh like the RHYWP?"

I said, "Us SPOBBs are not copycubs! No, we are just going to capture Mister Twister, rescue Smells from Spoiler, plus have a load of fun!"

So now our full short name is SPOBBTHALOF (**S**mall **P**ack **o**f **B**rute **B**easts **t**hat **H**ave **a** **L**oad **o**f **F**un). We did three loud Arrrroooos for it and quick as a chick, Stubbs made us all SPOBBTHALOF badges with his clever beak.

Plus, guess what? He did me a fancy T-shirt saying LITTLE WOLF, PACK LEADER on the chesty side!

Yours proudly,

Little Wolf, (PL)

P.S. Yeller wants us to do some short SPOBBTHALOF PAWBOOKS so I will send you 1 soonly, Ok?

Dear Mom and Dad,

Not much time to write because of Packtraining, but here is a bit of our Pawbook. Yeller did the writing, so it is fine and shouty, also quite hilly.

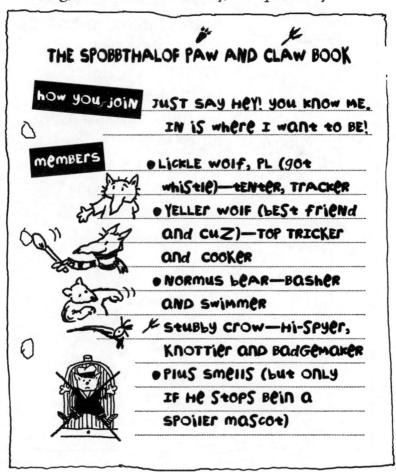

THE SPOBBTHALOF PAW AND CLAW BOOK

how you join — JUST SAY HEY! YOU KNOW ME, IN IS WHERE I WANT TO BE!

members
- LICKLE WOLF, PL (GOT WHISTLE)—TENTER, TRACKER
- YELLER WOLF (BEST FRIEND AND CUZ)—TOP TRICKER AND COOKER
- NORMUS BEAR—BASHER AND SWIMMER
- STUBBY CROW—HI-SPYER, KNOTTIER AND BADGEMAKER
- PLUS SMELLS (BUT ONLY IF HE STOPS BEIN A SPOILER MASCOT)

motto	BE speciaL

ruLes

- do not have 2 many rules (2 strikt)
- have a load of fun
- stick up for our motto
- have campin in tents, also in dens, shelters, and stuff like that
- NO RVS
- make things
- no doing arm burns on each other
- BETTER tricks than sticks (but normus gets first bash in emerjuncy)

watch this spAce

JUST in cASe,
of short New rule
(NOT sad but cool)

Did you like the "Claw" part of our Paw and Claw Book? Yeller put that in for Stubbs 'specially, because of crows not having normal paws.

Yours proudly,

Little Wolf, Pack Leader

Dear Mom and Dad,

I am sitting on a comfy molehill not far from Windy Ridge. And guess what? Our flag is UP, arrrrrrroooooo! Our 4-brute Pack Tent will be up soonly 2, I bet.

SPOBBTHALOF

But we did not go unplanningly from my house, oh no. 1st we did backpack packing. It was so hard because of tent poles, matches, bedrolls, tweezers, flashlights, pencils, frying pans, snacks, alphabetti spaghetti, plus cans of bakebeans (canteen size), I love them kiss kiss!

Also knife, fork, spoon, nets, glue, toggles, woggles, foggles, joggles, sleepybags, string, plus noodly pots, notebooks, bandages, kebab sticks, ect.

Normus's pack was a bit 2 big but then Stubbs made him take out the sofa, so a bit better.

Then off we went quickmarchingly through Frettnin Forest, going leftright leftright, searchy search for Smells, ect.

Where we are going is a secret so I will write it smally. Broken Tooth Caves, shhhh.

Yours blownaboutly,

Little

P.S. I forgot to say Y we are going to you know where. No time now. Maybe tomorrow, Ok?

Dear Mom and Dad,

Brrrr, blowy up here, plus dark as dark. Also, it
is hard to sleep so I am writing tiredoutly by
flashlight going flash.

Look, I have done you some pics of us doing
tents. That is me with the wissul.

This is our 1st try, it was bad, because only a
small shower curtain really.

This is our next try (Stubbs made it with his clever beak out of table cloth). Yes, it is a bit squashy, also Normus will not all go in.

Last night we did our 1st sleep-in-1-tent-practiss. The practiss was good but not the sleep. Stubbs says never mind, he can knit a nice shelter out of twigs for us (bit like a nest only other way upply) so maybe more snoozy. Also, 1 other good thing, I thought up some tent rules to go in the space in our Paw and Claw Books.

Tent Rules

- Normus, be careful, no rolling over on people, Ok?

- No bundling

- No itchy food

- No lickwashing after the gong of midnight

- Go to the bathroom before zipflaps time (but not in the tent, Ok?)

It's sunjumpup time now, so we are hunting small wigglers for breakfast. Then packing, then tracking!

Yours yawningly,

Laaaaaahtle (with a yawn, get it?)

Shrubbery bushy part, on the way across Dark Hills

Dear Mom and Dad,

Up and down we go marchingly today, over the Dark Hills. Look out, Broken Tooth Caves (sssshhh, remember), here comes the SPOBBTHALOFs! Oh yes, I was going to say before, Y we decided to go there. Ready? Here is Y.

We had a short campfire practiss before we went off packly. We had alphabetti spaghetti, hmmm nice! I did some writing in it like this.

Then round the campfire we played Branestorm, so our branes could have a strong think of sum ideas. I put them all down in my notebook like this:

1. Get Smells back quick. Where is he now? Answer: being Spoiler's mascot. ✓

2. Spoiler is after Mister Twister. BUT (big but) remember, Spoiler doesn't read anything proply, so he does not know about Mr. Twister's address off the poster. Plus Stubbs saw RV tracks near Hazardous Canyon. That means Spoiler is guessing where Mister Twister is, so probly he is going to have a look on Vile Isle or go more northly searching in the White Wildness or Yellowsmoke Swamplands. ✓

3. Do not chase RVs (2 speedy 4 us). ✓

4. Best to find Mister Twister and wait by him till Spoiler comes his way. ✓

5. Where is Mister Twister? Answer: not sure xactly. Oh yes, his address says "The Den, Broken Tooth Caves," but he is soooo crafty, maybe that is just a trick to trick packs! Never mind, we will go and look for clues there anyway. ✓

6. Hard part. Capture Mister Twister, then send out a message saying "Nar Nar Spoiler, what are you going to do about it?" (Normus's idea) ✓

7. Very hard part. When Spoiler comes, SPOBBS do an ambush on him and his RHYWP then uncapture smells. ◄

The End

Must go now to do secret tracking ~~sing sine~~
sign practiss, just in case of somewun getting lost,
ect.

For xample,

That means "Smells went that way," get it?

Yours leadingly,

L.W. (PL)

Dear Mom and Dad,

I will say to you by tracking sign what we are doing. Now, if you did not say, "Ah-ha, that means Spread Out Everybody," then go in the corner with a pointy hat on saying Duncehead (only kidding, not really Dad).

I said to my pack, "Let us do Spreadouting just so we can go all around Mister Twister, then close in tight on him all of a suddenly. It will be like sharp teeth on a mice pie, what do you think, SPOBBs?" Then they said, "Oh, fine Pack Leading, Little!" so I am feeling all proud.

Stubbs is Spreadouting eastly for a good look over Vile Isle, ect. Yeller and Normus are Spreadouting 2 different ways over the Dark Hills. So guess where I am off 2? I am going straight up northly, across the Parching Plain, to see if I can spot fur or fluff of Mister Twister up near Borderlands Market.

Yours offwetrottly,

L. Wolf

Dear Mom and Dad,

I am in the Parching Plain, it is hot as hot but not 1 pool or stream to wet my tongue in. Also, you get sharp thorns and stones in your pads, plus 2 claws bust, boo shame.

The best thing is the wind going *woooooo,* but not the dust, it gets up your smellholes. Not many big hungry birds have come flicking me with their shadows. Good thing because I forgot to bring Yeller's kite, the 1 with eyes painted on it, so no going flip and flap in their ugly face. Never mind, I have got out my tentpole. Now if they try making a snack out of me, I will give them a shocking poke with the pointy end.

Sometimes you see some scaly crawlers going wiggle, but no large brute beasts yet. BUT (big but) I have found some dinosaur tracks like this.

I am having a wonder, is it that crafty fox in a clever dizgizze? (Cannot spell it.) Off I go.

Yours warmly,

The Panter

Dear Mom and Dad,

You know that dinosaur?
It was not Mister Twister, plus
it was not a dinosaur. It was a
nostrich! He is funny, no fur
at all. He is like a grate big
feathery ball, plus tall bare
legs with just skin on, plus his
neck is like the hose on my
vacuum cleaner!

I said, "Hello, I am Little Wolf, have you seen a
crafty fox called Mister Twister by any chance?"
Then guess what? He went "Uh-oh" all of a
suddenly and stuck his head down a hole.

I said, "Sorry to interrupt, are you looking for a snack?" Then his tall legs went all twitchy and I thought, "Look out, he might give me a hard kick!" But no, he just said back (muffly voice), "Thank you. Call again, Mister Wolf, I am not at home today."

I said replyingly, "Good joke! But do not fret and fear, I want a nice ride not a nostrich stew. Can you take me to Borderlands Market before the sun drops behind the Murky Mountains?"

He said tremblingly, "If I was at home, I would like to, certainly, oh yes. But I have gone away to a dark place where nostriches are safe from danger."

I had a dig in my backpack, then quick as a chick I pulled out his head and popped a sock on it.

So now he has got his nerve up again, ready for riding! More tomorrow.

Yours yeeharly,

Cowboy Wolf

P.S. Maybe it was my sore eyes plus dusty white fur made the nostrich think I was an old danger, huh? I must write that trick down in my notebook for Yeller, it is a handy 1, Arrrrooo!

Here I am in Borderlands Market sorebottomly. I went bong-bong-bong-bong-bongly across the Parching Plain on the back of a nostrich's neck all the way. But between the bongs, I said to myself, "I know, Mister Twister likes taking money from people! So praps I will go 2 the market and have a look around for him." I have parked my nostrich in the bicycle rack just near

Mom and Dad
The Lair
Murkshire

the river. Now he is pecking up the nice pawful of pebbles I gave him for his supper. I think I will have a curlup myself under a small bench

Little X

Dear Mom and Dad,

Me wunce morely, near the end part of this day.

Soon after sunjumpup, I woke up thinking.
"Wait! Sposing I do see fur and fluff of that fox!
He is so crafty he might see me 1st. What shall I
dress up as?" *Ding* came an idea, so I jumped
splashingly in the river to get my dust off, then I
fluffed up my fur and put my bandana on my
neck for a collar. Then off I went pant-pant,
pant-pant by many a lampost saying "wuff wuff"
(me, not the lamppost). I was feeling a bit
starving but not
for long because
of all the people
going, "Ahhhhh,
nice puppy, pat-
pat, have a doggy
snack."

It was nice,
but when I was near the marketplace, guess
what? Across the road I ran swiftly, not looking.
All of a suddenly, a loud EEEEEK! came to my

ears from a van. Oh no, it was trying to kill me dead!

The old lady driving was all upset and nasty 2 me. She showed me her sharp teeth, then waved her fist. Funny, because the hairs on her head were gray, but the hairs on her fist were red! Then she put her bonnet back on straight and away she went brrrrmmmly. The name on the side of the van was MRS. GENTLY'S FURRY BOOT CO. So I said a joke to that van, I said, "Your driver does not look very Gently to me, get it?"

Now I think I must leave this town, it is 2 dangerous for a small cub here.

Yours narrowsqueakly,

Littly

Sack of ~~puttatoh, pottytoes~~ spuds,
Veggie Stall, the marketplace, Borderlands Market

Dear Mom and Dad,

Good thing I parked that nostrich. Do you know Y? Because that Mrs. Gently was not a nice old market lady in a bonnet, not at all!

I crept spyingly into the marketplace, hiding among the legs, also behind fruit and veggies. Then I saw a small crowd gathered around the back of a van. I peeped out behind a small herd of onions wonderingly. I heard a soft voice say, "My dears! I observe that many of your feet are clad only in the thinnest of shoes. How will you protect them from the sharp frosts and snows when winter comes? Allow me to recommend my beautiful Bunnyfur Boots. Step up and look into my eyes while I tell you how cheap and cheering they are."

Straight away, all the people opened up their purses saying, "Help yourself, dear lady. I must have a pair of those beautiful Bunnyfur Boots! My footwear is so inadequate, ect." And do you know what? I saw that old lady bend down from the back of her van taking all their money! Then the wind blew her dress up at the back showing her gingery tail, plus blowing a sharp smell of pepper up my nose. So I said, "Oh no, it is Mister Twister, my Foe! He stole those furry boots off our rabbits in Frettnin Forest, I bet!"

Yours sherlockly,

Detective Wolf

P.S. Grrrr, now I will be like spitted out chewy gum in a fox's tail (hard 2 see, hard to shake off).

Treeline, Mountain Track, Middle Slopes,
Outlaw Peak, Beastshire

Dear Mom and Dad,

It is good having a nostrich in desert places,
they are fast gallopers. Plus it is good fun going
bong-bong, ect., so you shake your head off
nearly. I am tracking Mister Twister. He packed
up quick from the market with a big bag of
money. Off he went driving his van eastly. He
was a fast brrrmer, but not as speedy as a nostrich
because of the road being a rough 1. Soon I was
sure he was going to Broken Tooth Caves, so I
pointed my nostrich off the road. I wanted to go
around the back (a bit northly), then climb up
Outlaw Peak to have a fine lookout place for
my SPOBBs.

When the path started being
2 hilly for my nostrich, off his
neck I jumped. I let him keep
my sock for his shyness (saves
looking for holes), plus I let
him eat my woggle, my toggle,
my foggle, and my joggle to stop

his tummy going rumble. He said humbly, "Good-bye, nice carrying you, you are very fierce but fair."

Up the steep track I went puffingly, keeping a sharp smellout all on my ownly for wolfscent or bearpong plus looking for secret signs. It was not long before I came to some low trees and yessss! A secret sign! It was a sort of a bird, like a fat chicken or a small nostrich maybe. Then came a shocking SMACK on my head by a low branch. So I thought, "Now I know what that secret sign means. It does not mean 'Chickens coming' or 'Do you like nostriches?' No, it means 'DUCK!'" (Normus is a fine trout tickler, but he is not so hot at pics.)

That is all for now,

Yours seeingstarsly,

Bonkhead Boy

Dear Mom and Dad,

My next secret sign that I found was this.

I found where the track turned just under a cliff, like a high wall. I went Grrrrr because of its meaning "You are a small weaky, you are like bubbles." But I found out all of a suddenly it was not a rude sign, because an echo made my GRRRRRR come back very loud 4 times, plus a load of rocks (lairsize) came roaring avalanchely. Lucky I fell flat or no head left! That was how I found out what that sign means really. It means **"SSSSSSSHHH! AvALANCHES!"** (Boo shame.)

I did a short note in my notebook for more secret tracking sign practiss, then up I went more steeply with my eyes going flick, in case of more danger. The next secret sign was more true. It was like this.

It meant, "Watch it, take the wiggly path going right," so I did. And it was a good 1, so well done you SPOBBs!

I have just stopped for a short pant and a letter.

Yours reportingly,

Little

Dear Mom and Dad,

Arrrooooo! I have found 2 SPOBBs at last. After a dark, cold, lone walk to the top of Outlaw Peak, up the other side they came strugglingly!

Yeller whispered loudly, "HELLO, PL! NORMUS AND ME HAVE NOT FOUND MISTER TWISTER BUT WE HAVE MADE A FINE DISCOVERY!"

I said, "Well done, Yeller. Did you find Spoiler and Smells?"

He said replyingly, "NO, BUT DID YOU DETECT MISTER TWISTER?"

97

I said, "Do not fret and frown, I saw him at Borderlands Market. He will be coming here soonly, I bet. Tell me about the fine discovery you made."

So Yeller said, "WE SEARCHED ALL AROUND BROKEN TOOTH CAVES, SNEAKIN AND PEEKIN IN MANY A DARK TUNNEL AND DODGIN MANY A CRAFTY TRAP. THEN AT LAST WE FOUND **THE DEN!**"

DEN

Normus said addingly, "Yeah, but shame that crafty fox was not at home. I wanted to bash him. What was he doing at Borderlands Market?"

So I said about Mrs. Gently selling furry boots, ect., and Normus said, "Ah-ha! So that was why he wanted those bunnies from Frettnin Forest, to bash them and steal their fur."

Yeller shouted another Ah-ha saying, "THAT EXPLAINS THE TRICK RABBICK HOLE WE FOUND DOWN BELOW BY MISTER TWISTER'S DEN. A SIGN OUTSIDE SAYS "FREE CARROTS. HOP IN FOR A NIBBLE." AT FIRST IT LOOKED JUST LIKE ANY OLD BURROW, BUT WHEN WE PEEPED IN WITH OUR FLASHLIGHTS GOIN FLASH, WE SAW LOADS AND LOADS OF RABBICKS ALL IN SACKS, PEEPIN OUT BLINKINLY."

I said (Pack Leader voice), "SPOBBS, pay attention. It is our job to let those rabbits go. We must send them back to Frettnin Forest where they belong. They need their own holes to hop into. Also, it is not fair them being chased by strangers. They want to be chased by us locals, so they can be normal rabbit pies, not furry boots."

So down we went rushingly to that trick hole. We unsacked the rabbits and sent them back home scamperingly to Frettnin Forest.

Yours fairly,

Little

P.S. Now we must shut our eyes and think skweezingly about what is keeping Mr. Twister from coming back 2 his den. Also, has Stubbs found Spoiler and Smells yet?

Dear Mom and Dad,

Woke up this morning, our tent all white with
snow because so high up (snow is Yeller's worst
thing, it makes him tremble). But after a warm
cookup on our fire (stones all around to stop
flames spreading, hem hem), we heard a flippy
flap plus a long lost "Ark" that made us all more
cheery wunce morely. It was Stubbs!

He said "Ark!" meaning Hark, could we hear
the engine of Spoiler's RV that he had been
following? Answer: Yes! So out with our fire,
down with our tent, and off we all crawled
peepingly through the sharp
white grasses, down the side
of the mountain. Way below
we saw Broken Tooth
Caves plus down farther in
the valley, the road going
wiggle. The snow did not
reach there, so the RV went
nippingly. It was like a small
toy bus, stopping close by
the turnoff to the caves.

Out jumped Spoiler plus Smells having a piggy back. Also all the Really Harshies. Then we heard a *brrrm-pop-pop-bang* coming the other way. It sounded like Uncle after he'd eaten all the bakebeans, but it was Mister Twister with engine trouble! That was Y he was going along creepingly like a snail.

Quick as chicks, the RHYWP made a pretend avalanche and blocked the road by a bend so Mister Twister's van had to stop. Then guess what? They did an ambush and captured him! Yes, true, honest! Mister Twister got captured and *not* by the SPOBBs, so shaming!

Yours shockedly,

L. Wolf

Dear Mom and Dad,

This is me. I am hiding in the bushes with the SPOBBTHALOFs outside the lectric fence around Spoiler's RV. Sad to say, there is no way in for us yet.

The RHYWP is a big showoff, singing loud ambush songs like:

> Mister Twister's in a box,
> He is just a weaky fox.
> Fame is what we all will win,
> When we go and turn him in!
>
> He was such a smartypaw.
> He thought he could beat the law!
> Spoiler's boys soon put him right.
> He will make us rich tonight!

Oh Yah, so smart are we!
The Really Harsh Young WP!
We came, we saw, and then we scored.
Now we get a fat reward!

PUSH! PUSH! AMBUSH!

SPOILER PACK LEADER

Then they had to stop because of Smells, you know what he is like when he gets jealous of not getting patted. He opened up the engine cover of the RV and got in with his little hammer, playing "Bonk All the Bits."

Spoiler said, "Skyooz me, stop, Smellybreff! Stop *right now* or you will break it, OK yah?" So Smells said, "Only if you call me Big Fur."

So Spoiler said, "OK, Big Fur, but no bashing engines, all right?"

Then Smells said, "Piggyback, piggyback, piggyback, piggyback." He did not stop till he made all the RHYWP give him a good bouncy ride. Then he did a throw-up, saying, "Mommy Mommy."

We want to uncapture him quick, but 2 dangerous yet because of lectric shocks plus large guards.

Yours chewpenly,

Dear Mom and Dad,

Today Yeller had 1 of his best Big Ideas ever. It is called the Trojan Moose! So we gathered all grass plus twiggy stuff plus bits of string, then Stubbs got busy with his clever beak. He knitted a big huge moose like this with a trick door in it, plus room for Normus to hide in.

This is our new plan.

1. Give the RHYWP a big shock by Normus
2. Steal Mister Twister from Spoiler
3. Uncapture Smells
4. Claim huge reward for Mister Twister
5. Get back the proud name of Wolf and say "Well done, you SPOBBS!"

When the sun hid behind the Dark Hills, we pushed the Trojan Moose on his wheels and left him outside the lectric fence of the RHYWP camp.

When we got near the RV, we could hear Smells inside talking to Spoiler. Spoiler was trying to have a zizz so they had a little chat starting with Smells:

"Spoiler?"

"OK yah, Big Fur. What do you want?"

"Spoiler?"

"Yah?"

"Spoiler?"

"What do you want?"

"Spoiler?" ect.

Good, huh? That means he has not changed 1 bit since he went off to be a mascot. He is still ~~a~~ ~~noosance~~ ~~nuisince~~ newsen his normal painy self.

Yours waitingly,

yore Special PL

Dear Mom and Dad,

At sunjumpup today, us SPOBBs were
listening from our hidyplaces. When we heard the
RHYWP guards
talking, all our eyes
went peep.

The guards said
headscratchingly, "Hey,
what is that? Looks like
some cool statue type
thing, huh? Be careful,
man, yah? Leave it,
maybe. Could be a
threat, what d'you think?
Check it out with Spoiler,
right, yah?" ect.

Then we heard Smells saying tantrumly, "No!
Me want it! Big Fur want to play wid da moosy!"

Spoiler came out of the RV yawningly, saying,
"Oh, bring it in, it's only some big toy. Let
Smellybreff play with it, for howling out loud!
Anything's better than having to play 'Ga Ga Goo'

again, yah?" So the guards turned off the lectric, and pushed the Trojan Moose inside the fence.

Soon Smells was more cheery playing "Giddy Up Moosy to the Fair," plus making all the guards say, "Giddy Up, Big Fur!"

Stubbs said a whisper "Ark!" meaning *Ark*splain what "Ga Ga Goo" is. So I said 2 him how it is 1 of Smells's best games. He has to be the Mommy with the lipstick, then you have to lie down and be the Big Baby and let him feed you mud stew by a bottle.

Now it is getting late. Yeller, me, and Stubbs are a bit wurrid, case Normus gets bashed or captured by all the strong Harshies. What if they all gang up on him? Will he get the biggest arm burn ever?

Your nervous,

Number 1 Cub

The RV (captured by the SPOBBTHALOFs)

Dear Mom and Dad,

Whyo Y did I fret and frown about Normus?
He is a mighty hero and a Big Shocker!

1st he waited till Smells got bored of "Giddy
Up Moosy." That was when Smells said, "Who
wants to play 'Doctors' and let me do
injeckshuns!" Then all the guards went away
zoomingly to hide behind the RV.

Quick as a chick, out jumped
Normus with a big
GROWL! He ripped
the front wheel off the
RV. That gave all the
Harshies a nasty shock,
so they packed together
showing their sharp
teeth. Then they
shouted "PUSH!
PUSH! AMBUSH!"
Spoiler was in the front
of the attack, all bristly
and big as a buffalo!

But Normus was not scared 1 bit. He closed
1 eye and rolled that tire bowlingly at them. That
made them turn the other way sharp! They all
went, "HELP! HELP! WIPE-OUT!" Then they
went BOING over the lectric fence like scaredy
kangaroos.

Me and Yeller were waiting on the other side
with Mister Twister's rabbit sacks and in the
Harshies went plop plop plop plop! They could not
get out again because Stubbs tied them up quick
with special SPOBB ~~nkots~~ ~~nots~~ knots by his clever
beak! Spoiler wanted to jump the fence like the
rest of the RHYWP, but he was the last 1. That is Y
he got squished by a front tire bowling him over,
shame, huh? Not really, ARRRRRRROOOOO!

Now I 'spect his mom will say, "What Ho, you
flat young cowpat, have you seen our darling
grate big harsh cub called Spoiler?" And he will
say, "Blub blub, Mommy, it is me."

Yours 'specially,
ARkela of SPOBBS (Stubbs idea)

Dear Mom and Dad,

Just a short letter today because of being busy with our prisoners. We are keeping Spoiler in the lickroom of the captured RV. He is coming unsquished in a slow way, so looking like his normal beautiful hansum self (only kidding, not really).

Mister Twister is still captured 2. BUT (big but) we cannot claim our huge reward because he is in the secret cell and Spoiler will not say the combination of the secret panel to me. Boo shame! Spoiler keeps saying smarmly, "Skyooz me, listen up, Little Wolf. Y don't we PLs just agree to split the large reward for arresting Mister Twister? I mean, isn't that fairnuff, yah? OK, so, you just release me and my pack, then I will give you the combination, and we can all go along to the police station and get really, really wealthy. Good plan, yah?"

Yours notsurewhattodonextly,

Little

P.S. Smells is fine only he keeps snuggling up to Spoiler's door going "Numb-ah numb-ah numb-ah numb-ah." Just because he wants to see Mister Twister and say "Nar Nar" 2 him I bet.

Dear Mom and Dad,

Do not go mad and get your temper up, but Mister Twister has done a fast getaway. This is how.

Me, Yeller, and Stubbs were outside the RV watching Normus bash the wheel back on the front. Smells came down the steps of the RV with eyes wide as windows plus big naughty smile. Also, he was hiding something behind his back. He looked at Normus in a crafty way. "Have you put da wheel back on, Normus?" Then Normus said, eyerollingly, "Yes, Smells, this round thing is the wheel. It is not off any more. That is cos of me bashing it back ON, is that clear?"

Then, all of a rushly, Mister Twister jumped up behind Smells and pushed him off the steps! He shut the driver's door of the RV thuddingly.

Then he started up the engine, shouting, "Such a pity, my boys! I must leave you in a hurry. Consider yourselves OUTFOXED!" Then off he went screechingly, going *beep beep*, dustcloud dustcloud.

All of us SPOBBs did a pretend sob and waved bye-bye. Then we jumped upanddownly, doing our pack Arrroooo! times 3 for cheeryness!

Yours hi5ly,

L. Wolf

P.S. I forgot to say about Stubbs going "Ark" meaning Arksplain what you are hiding behind your back, smells. Answer, moneybag moneybag moneybag, mine mine mine!

Dear Mom and Dad,

Thank you for your present of a large empty shoebox plus string so Smells can make a nice package and send all his money to you. Yes, I will ask nicely but you know what a big miser he is.

You say in your note, "Say fine work to him and kiss his darling fluffy cheeks for Mommy." Plus you say to me, "Never darken our lair door again, also deliver yourself a sharp clip on the ear for going loony. You are hopeless and have let down our proud name of Wolf, as usual, while giving the Snarl-Wolfingtons loads to sneer about!"

But Mom and Dad, Y are you so crool? You do not understand! Mister Twister was not the winner! Listen, I will tell you the score, it is:

MISTER Twister, zIP
SPOBBTHALOFS 999999999 millium
Spoiler plus RHYWP, zip
SPOBBTHALOFS 9999999 millium
millivms

But you will not even listen how we did it , I
bet, so I am all upset. Plus, I am going home with
a stampy stamp.

Your sulkingly,

Not Telling

Dear Mom and Dad,

Ah-ha! I can see from your gloating note saying, "Arrrooooo and Nar Nar, the Snarl-Wolfingtons have done a moonlight sneak-away with their tails between their legs," that you are feeling a lot more cheery today!

So merci (French) for writing, also for Dad's spy-photo of Mister Twister's letter that he sent to them.

118

Dear Mr. and Mrs. Snarl-Wolfington,

I have recently turned the tables on your precious Spoiler by single-handedly capturing him and his entire pack of Really Harsh Young Wolves. They surrendered to me without a struggle and I have them all tied up in sacks in their fine RV that I have confiscated to replace my old van. Harsh? I have known frogspawn harsher than your son.

May I suggest that you sell your mansion immediately and send the money you get for it to me? I feel sure that you will wish to do this speedily before your neighbors, Grizzle and Gripper, find out what a complete mess your only cub made of his attempt to capture me and become famous.

Yours smugly,

Mister Twister the Fox

Also, Mom and Dad, you say you are grrring to know how this arrroooooey thing happened. Oh, all right, then, I will tell you a nice story. It is called "How Little Wolf, Pack Leader of the SPOBBs, beat Spoiler plus Mister Twister in 1 shot." Ready?

How Little Wolf, Pack Leader of the SPOBBs, Beat Spoiler plus Mister Twister in 1 shot.
By L. Wolf.

Wunce upon an RV, there was a very small bad cub called Smells. He was always getting on everywun's nerves going, "Numb-ah numb-ah numb-ah numb-ah," ect., all the time in people's ears. Well, do you know a funny thing? There was a grate, huge, hot-shot cub called Spoiler Snarl-Wolfington who was PL of the RHYWP. He had grate, big, sharp teeth and all big mussels. BUT (big but) he was not like Little Wolf and his SPOBBs who were used to Smells going on and on. So after only about ten hours, Spoiler gave in saying, "Please, I'll do anything you want, OK yah?" So Smells made him whisper the combination of his secret cell to him.

Then Smells's hansum big bro Little Wolf guessed something was up, so he said, "Come on, baby bro, what did

Spoiler whisper? You can tell me, you are in my pack really." But Smells just shook his head going *pppppppppprrrr* with his lips.

So Little Wolf found out the answer in a very crafty way. First he did a whisper to Normus saying, "Normus, you go and bash the wheel back on the RV." Then Little Wolf did another whisper to Yeller (his best friend and cuz) saying, "Go and put the RV driving keys in the driving keyhole." Then Little Wolf went, "Psss wsss, ect.," in Stubbs's ear just to make Smells jealous.

Smells said, "Give ME a whisper!" So Little Wolf said, "OK, Big Fur, I will." He whispered to him, "Whatever you do, you must never never never stand outside the secret door and say to Mr. Twister, 'Hello in there. If you give me your bag of money, I will open the door to the secret room by a secret combination.'"

And Smells said replyingly, "OK, I promise." Then off he trotted gigglingly with his paw over his smile.

Soon, off the RV jumped Little Wolf, Pack Leader, plus the SPOBBs. They did not have to wait long before OUT came Smells with his eyes wide as windows hiding the moneybag behind his back. Then off drove Little Wolf's foxy foe in the RV with Spoiler plus the RHYWP in the back!

Yours happyeverafterly,

The Storyteller

Dear Mom and Dad,

We are packing up our Pack Tent today and getting ready to go back to Frettnin Forest for a proper old-fashy rabbit hunt. Arrrrroooo!

Our sleep last night was the longest yet, hmm nice, because Smells wanted to have his sleep in the Trojan Moose, handy huh? He helped us get ready (in a way) by chewing through all the tent ropes before we woke up.

Can you send him a photo of Dad saying "No weeing on fires?" We had to have our noodles a bit cold today all because of Smells liking the sound of HISSSSS. (Never mind, xtra rations of bakebeans to make up, I love them kiss kiss.)

Yours goinghomely,

Little

Comfy Armchair

Dear Mom and Dad,

Thank you for your letter saying well done in teeny small letters, I know it hurt.

Dad says he does not understand Y we did not just drive Mister Twister to the police and claim the huge reward like any normal wolf would have done.

Answer (in Yeller's words, the same wuns he said to Normus when he asked that kwestion): "YES, BUT WHAT A BIG SHAME IF WE TAKE HIM TO THE PLEECE. THEN WE WON'T HAVE ANY PROPER ENEMIES IN FRETTNIN FOREST AND THAT IS NOT RIGHT, LICKLE!

125

WHERE IS THE CHALLENGE FOR US
SPOBBS IF OUR BEST CRAFTY FOE IS
AWAY BEIN A CONVICT?"

See? We like crafty foes to
help us sharpen up our tricks!

Now I will say adios, I am off to chase rabbits,
also to stuff wool up my ears. Did I say that Smells
made me send off Mister Twister's moneybag for a
drum kit? I was hoping he would find a nice quiet
craze instead of being a drummer in a rock band,
but no luck. All because of Mister Twister saying
he was a star, just for opening the door of his
secret cell. Boo shame.

Yours deffly,

L. Wolf, PACK LEADER